DISCARD

Rosa Raposa

F. Isabel Campoy

ILLUSTRATED BY
Jose Aruego
AND **Ariane Dewey**

Gulliver Books
Harcourt, Inc.

San Diego   New York   London

To Alma Flor Ada,
my favorite storyteller
—F. I. C.

For Juan
—J. A. and A. D.

Requests for permission to make copies of any part of the work should be mailed to the following address:
Permissions Department, Harcourt, Inc., 6277 Sea Harbor Drive, Orlando, Florida 32887-6777.

www.HarcourtBooks.com

Gulliver Books is a trademark of Harcourt, Inc., registered in the United States of America
and/or other jurisdictions.

Library of Congress Cataloging-in-Publication Data
Campoy, F. Isabel.
Rosa Raposa/by F. Isabel Campoy; illustrated by Jose Aruego and Ariane Dewey.
p. cm.
"Gulliver Books."
Summary: A wily fox outwits Jaguar in three trickster tales set in the jungles of South America.
[1. Foxes—Fiction. 2. Jaguar—Fiction. 3. Tricksters—Fiction. 4. Jungles—Fiction.
5. South America—Fiction.] I. Aruego, Jose, ill. II. Dewey, Ariane, ill. III. Title.
PZ7.C16153Ro 2002
[E]—dc21 2001005322
ISBN 0-15-202161-2

First edition
A C E G H F D B
Manufactured in China

The illustrations in this book were made with pen and ink,
gouache, watercolor, and pastel on Strathmore Kit paper.
The display type was set in Big Dog.
The text type was set in Cloister Oldstyle.
Color separations by Bright Arts Ltd., Hong Kong
Manufactured by South China Printing Company, Ltd., China
This book was printed on totally chlorine-free Nymolla Matte Art paper.
Production supervision by Sandra Grebenar and Pascha Gerlinger
Designed by Lydia D'moch

A Note from the Author

My mother was a great storyteller who loved to tell me Spanish trickster tales about a fox who always gets the best of a wolf. In *Rosa Raposa*, I have moved the setting of her tales from Spain to the Brazilian jungle and changed the wolf into a jaguar.

The story takes place in the Amazon Rainforest, near the Amazon River in South America.

A few things Rosa Raposa comes across in the Amazon Rainforest:

Chango-monkey	*Chango* is the word for monkey in some Latin American countries.
maracuya	The fruit of a maracuya vine, also called passion fruit; often used to make a sweet drink.
liana	A tropical climbing plant with the strength and flexibility of a cord.
jaguar	The biggest feline in the Americas and a great hunter; usually hunts at night.

A Cry for Help

Except for the troublesome presence of Jaguar, Rosa Raposa loved her life in the jungle. As long as she stayed far away from Jaguar's beady eyes and sharp yellow teeth, most days were peaceful.

But one afternoon a cry rang through the trees. "Help! Help! Can anyone hear?"

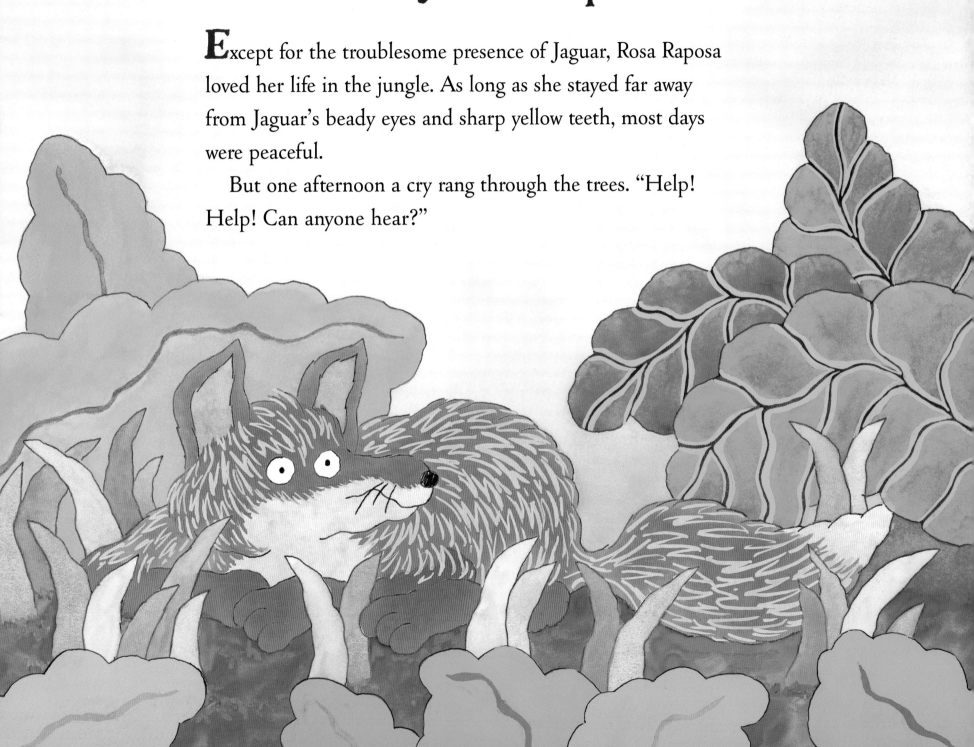

Rosa Raposa ran toward the voice, but her friend Chango-monkey got there first.

"Ha!" said Chango-monkey. "Jaguar is trapped. Perhaps we should leave him there. The jungle will be much safer."

"Don't be afraid of me!" said Jaguar.
"I beg you. Please help me out of here!
I'll give you all the bananas you can eat."

Chango-monkey could not resist bananas. "Well...," he said.
And to Rosa Raposa's surprise, Chango-monkey set Jaguar free.

"Poor, ridiculous Chango-monkey! Don't you know me
better than that?" said Jaguar once he was free. "Being
stuck in that hole made me hungry." And he grabbed
Chango-monkey.

"Wait," Rosa called. "Didn't Chango-monkey help you?"

Jaguar hesitated before saying, "No…no he didn't. I
jumped out by myself."

"Wow, Jaguar, you must be a very strong and capable jumper. Show me where you were, please," said Rosa Raposa.

Jaguar puffed up his fur proudly. "Oh yes, I am," he said. Then he jumped into the hole. "See? I was down here."

"You jumped up from all the way down there? I am very impressed."

Jaguar puffed up more. "Plus," he said, "that rock was on top of me!"

"Which rock? This one?" asked Rosa.

"Yes! That one! Show her, Chango-monkey!"

Rosa and Chango-monkey quickly pushed the rock back over the hole, trapping Jaguar again.

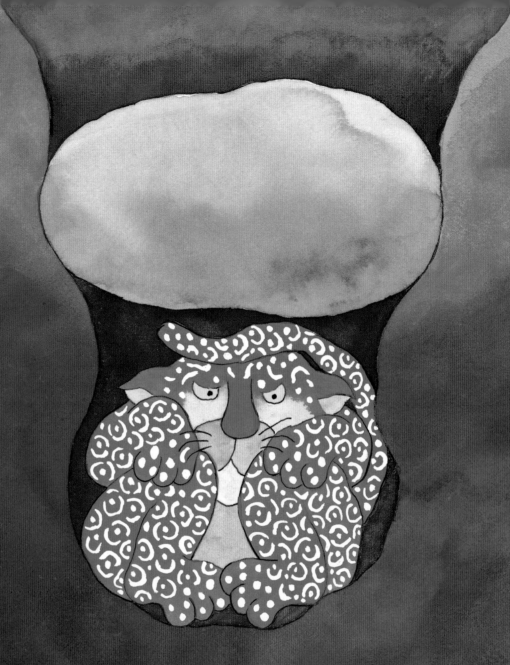

Then Rosa and Chango-monkey left, singing:

"Beware of Jaguar's tears.
And even if he calls for help,
Never get very near."

A Strong North Wind

Rosa Raposa was having the time of her life. Jaguar had been out of sight for several weeks, and Rosa had been playing freely throughout the jungle.

"I'm a bird, and I can fly high up to the sky," Rosa sang while swinging from a liana.

Suddenly, two yellow eyes peered through the leaves. A spotted tail flashed on the branch. Oh no—it was Jaguar!

Rosa thought quickly. "Oh, Jaguar, thank goodness you're here. Could you help me tie myself to this tree?" she asked in a frightened voice.

"But why?" growled Jaguar.

"Didn't you feel that breeze? A cyclone is coming. The winds will be so strong that they could blow me away from the jungle to…to…I don't know where!" said Rosa, almost crying.

Jaguar scratched his forehead.

Rosa pulled the liana, and some leaves fell on Jaguar's head. "Hurry! Hurry! The cyclone is almost here. Tie me to this tree!" she begged.

"Can you tie me first?" cried Jaguar.
"I don't want to be blown away, either."

"Well, all right," said Rosa, and she began to tie Jaguar to the tree. "Is this tight enough?"

"A little bit tighter," Jaguar said.

When Jaguar was completely tied up,
Rosa Raposa started to laugh. Then she set
off, singing:

> *"Beware of Jaguar's bite.*
> *And if you want to be safe,*
> *Always tie him very tight!"*

The Green Dress

It had not rained in a long time. Rosa Raposa longed for a drink of cool water and a swim. But Jaguar was very angry. She knew he was waiting for her by the river. So, she spent her days sitting under the maracuya vine, moaning:

"There is no water in the lakes.
There is no water in the ponds.
I think I will die of thirst."

"Come to the river. There is water there," said a passing crocodile.

"I can't. Jaguar is waiting for me there," Rosa moaned.

"Come to the river. There is water there," said a passing snake.

"I can't. Jaguar is waiting for me there," Rosa moaned even more.

Just then, a bee flew by Rosa's nose. She watched it fly up to a huge beehive among the branches.

"I have an idea," she said to herself. Rosa lured the bees out of the hive with a bunch of wildflowers. Then she climbed up into the maracuya vines and collected a bundle of leaves.

She stuck each leaf in the beehive, one by one, until all the leaves were coated in honey.

Next, she put leaves all over her fur, until she was completely covered.

Just then, several of the bees returned to their hive and
flew at Rosa's honey-covered face. Hidden in her green dress,
and chased by the angry bees, she hurried to the river.

Rosa Raposa saw Jaguar up ahead. "Uh-oh," she said quietly, and froze on the spot. As the furious bees caught up with her, Jaguar looked in her direction.

"What a strange tree that is," he said.

Rosa stood very still, both eyes fixed on one of the bees in front of her nose. Just as Jaguar finally looked away, the bee stung Rosa. "Ouch!" she cried, as she batted the bee away from her.

Jaguar looked back in her direction.

Rosa stood paralyzed. She longingly eyed the river as another bee approached her ear.

"That must be a maracuya vine. Their leaves always attract bees," Jaguar said. And he turned to listen to the river jumping from rock to rock.

"Ah—ah—achoo!" sniffed Rosa, startling the bee into stinging her right on the ear. Rosa held her breath in pain.

Jaguar lazily looked Rosa's way again. "My, those bees are noisy," he said, and turned his eyes away.

Rosa heard a loud buzzing behind her. She could not stand her thirst or the bee stings any longer. She took a huge leap right into the river, just as a large swarm of bees flew at her.

She drank and drank and drank as the bees circled above her.

As Rosa drank, the river began to pull away her leaves one by one.

"How did that maracuya vine get into the river?" Jaguar said. "And why is it losing its leaves?" Jaguar approached the river quietly.

Rosa stopped drinking to breathe. She looked around.
She saw leaves floating down the stream and a cloud of bees
right above her. And she saw Jaguar's eyes fixed on her.
"It's *you!*" Jaguar cried.

Taking a deep breath, Rosa dived under the water and swam
as fast as she could.

The bees looked around for Rosa. They couldn't find her,
but they *did* see Jaguar. Just as Jaguar was about to jump
into the river, the swarm of bees fell upon him.

When Rosa Raposa got to the other side of the river,
she saw Jaguar desperately trying to escape the bees. She
laughed, waved her one remaining leaf, and sang:

"Beware of a floating tree,
It could be a dress of leaves
Made with the help of bees."

"I hope I don't see you again," Rosa called across the river.

"Oh, you will, Rosa Raposa, you will,"
called Jaguar. Then he disappeared into
the trees, chased by the angry bees.